DRAGON TEA

CONNOR WHITELEY

No part of this book may be reproduced in any form or by any electronic or mechanical means. Including information storage, and retrieval systems, without written permission from the author except for the use of brief quotations in a book review.

This book is NOT legal, professional, medical, financial or any type of official advice.

Any questions about the book, rights licensing, or to contact the author, please email connorwhiteley@connorwhiteley.net

Copyright © 2022 CONNOR WHITELEY

All rights reserved.

DEDICATION
Thank you to all my readers without you I couldn't do what I love.

DRAGON TEA

Stretching his back, Cato felt his aching bones and muscles release all sorts of painful tension as he stood up after hours of leaning over the immense wooden table in front of him. He knew he shouldn't have stood in one place for so long but this is too important. He had to find out how the orks were getting this far into the Realm.

As Cato looked at the massive parchment map in front of him, he admired all of its black chaotic lines that tried to keep up with an ever-changing Realm. From the rich forests of the east and the Midlands to the harsh deserts of the far south. This map attempted to map it all.

Yet Cato knew that was impossible for any map maker. For it was a sad truth that the Realm lost and gain land every single day. Whether it be from the war with the orks or the dwarfs or any other creature that inhabited this world.

Moving away from that damn map for a moment, Cato gave his eyes a rest and attempted to admire the limited range of art he had on the cold stone walls of this hut. He always appreciated good art and Cato smiled a little as he remembered the bargaining he had to do to get a stunning painting of the breathtaking capital in the far North. That had to be his favourite.

But besides from that this hut like everything in this Dragon Rider training facility was empty. Just another forgotten corner of the Realm where people only paid attention to this place when they wanted something. Even if they just want to get rid of a problem.

Even now Cato laughed at the fact his father had banished him here for being gay and kicked out the army. Of course, it was their loss and at least these trainees could learn from the Lord Dragon Rider himself. The best rider in the Realm.

The smell of freshly cooked rabbit stew that already filled his mouth with the taste of sweet juicy rabbit, drew his attention away from the painting and the stupid map as Cato realised he had spent the entire day in here with nothing to show for his time. Maybe except having a day to himself without having to teach all the trainees about flying and dragon-riding. It was good to have a day off.

Then the sound of lots of claws hitting rock made Cato beam a little as he knew his dragonlets and trainees were home at last. He really hoped none of them were injured or anything bad happened. This was the first time in seven years he had allowed someone else to teach them their lessons. He hoped he wasn't going to regret letting Caden teach them.

Just saying his name made Cato smile a little and he felt his heart skip a few beats. He knew Caden would come in here later on and that would definitely be a welcomed distraction from the map.

He never would have admitted this to Caden but he was proving to be a useful addition to the facility. Cato never thought Caden would adapt so well to the mountains and become a good teacher, well liked by the trainees but he was.

Although, Cato was still unnerved by what his dragon Pendra had said to him. The memory was still fresh in his mind despite it being months ago. The only reason Caden was sent here was because his father had ordered it. To save him from being executed for treason and murder. Cato really needed to find out more because he would protect his trainees no matter the cost. And no matter how beautiful Caden was.

The sound of footsteps made Cato look towards the large opening where a door should have been attached to as Caden walked in. Cato really tried to stop a big smile from breaking out on his face. As he admired Caden's smooth elegant movements, his stunning longish blond hair that framed his sharp youthful face perfectly, and Caden's beautiful crystal blue eyes.

Caden gave him a beautiful smile as he passed Cato a cold metal cylindrical tankard of steaming black tea. As Cato touched the tankard's large metal handle, he made sure one of his fingers touched Caden's smooth hand for the briefest of moments.

A part of Cato wanted to kick himself for acting like this but he was right earlier when he said Caden would be a welcomed distraction.

Taking a big mouthful of the tea, Cato was instantly reminded why he was the only one who made his tea. Caden's tea tasted extremely bitter and disgusting. Even after he forced himself to swallow it, there was a horrific bitter aftertaste in his mouth. Cato made a mental note to give this disgusting tea to Pendra later for some reason dragons love bitter tea.

"Found anything," Caden asked in his beautiful velvety voice.

"Negative. The Orks live in the far, far north. Hence why the Lord Commander and King's forces are fighting all across the northern and eastern borders. But there is no way the orks could come this far south,"

"What about by ship and sailing down the Eastern coast?"

"Negative the elves patrol those waters too well. I remember my father telling me all sorts of fun tales where human vessels would be seized by elves,"

"Okay, what about crossing the western and southern borders?"

Cato had to laugh aloud at that point. Caden really was showing himself to be a military boy. A person uncultured and that suggestion alone showed he had been born and serving in the North his entire life.

"Do you really expect the dwarfs to allow orks to walk across their lands?"

Caden cocked his head for a moment. Probably trying to imagine a dwarf being kind or respectful to any non-dwarfs. Then he nodded in agreement.

"And the Southern border, I doubt the Trolls, witches and whatever creatures live there would allow some nice juicy orks to walk through,"

Cato frowned in frustration and his eyes narrowed at the map.

Caden wondered over and placed his arm over Cato's shoulders. Cato rolled his eyes that it wasn't lower.

"You'll figure it out. I believe in you,"

Cato started to feel like he would make a fool of himself so he asked "Where have our dragons gotten to?"

Caden rolled his eyes and withdraw the arm. Cato wondered if Caden wanted something to happen then?

"They're both debriefing the Dragonlets on today's training. I debriefed the human trainees too. They're up in the main hut having their dinner,"

Cato was about to ask him if he wanted to go for an evening ride with him and Pendra. But a loud burp gave from the doorway as this little fat lump of impressive blue scales walked, spat out a letter and started to fly out again.

Watching Caden's smooth and stunning movements as he walked, Cato always admired the variety of dragons there were in the world. From the majestic dragons like Pendra all the way down to the small delivery dragons. Even though he had to admit delivery dragons were some of the strangest dragons he knew.

When Caden walked back over, he stood so close to Cato that he could felt his pleasant body heat and Cato could smell the sweet oranges of the oil the Priestesses blessed the dragons with once a week. Presumably Caden had sat in some but Cato didn't have the mind power to think about those visiting Priestesses.

Cato saw Caden holding a little letter dripping with dragon spit. He took it out of Caden's hand and read it.

As he read the cold parchment letter, Cato could feel his mouth form a small smile at the words.

"What is it?"

"Caden, do you have some fine garments?"

"Ha. No,"

"I'll loan you some. It seems the Baroness Lawic has requested our presence,"

"Why? And how does the Baron thing work again?"

"Caden, what did you do growing up? Did you have any education in the real world?"

Caden took a step closer and said in his typical velvety voice. "I had an education. Then I enrolled in the army and fought orks for the rest of my life till a few months ago. I'm sorry I'm not as cultured as you. But I'm very good at other things you might be interested in,"

Cato took a step back.

"The King is the ruler of the Realm of course. But all land except the capital are run and looked after by the Barons and Baronesses. They are all appointed by the King and have absolute authority unless the King overrules them,"

Caden nodded.

"Why did she request our presence?"

"It seems like her Dragon Tea has been stolen and she wants our help getting it back,"

***

As the fresh night breeze of the city blow past Cato thought about how much he had missed the cities of the Realm. They were beautiful he remembered as he looked at the tall masonry buildings around him. With their immense blocks of rock shaped and moulded into whatever the Baroness desired.

Looking around Cato also remembered why he had never spent too long in cities even when his father had been there on business. As he saw a layer of straw over the disgusting muddy ground below and that was their road. Even worse, Cato saw a carriage full of human manure being carted through on the way to the field.

The smell was overwhelming and just plain disgusting. And it made his mouth taste foul. He wanted some water to wash away the taste. But Cato knew this was how the poor lived on the outskirts of the cities. It was the same all over the Realm.

Of course, he could go into the City to see the thousands of people and the nice tidy streets. But for some reason Pendra and Caden's dragon liked it here. And the Baroness was coming to them anyway.

Despite the disgusting smell, there wasn't anything wrong with the outskirts of the city. Everyone had their own room in these massive stone houses that formed part of the city's defences, and the little whispers of laughter and happiness was always a good bonus.

The sound of chaotic blowing made Cato turn away as he saw Pendra and Caden's dragon Kadien rapidly blowing on some straw they had lit. Cato hoped it was by accident.

Then looking at the two dragons in the bright white moonlight was a pleasure all by itself. Just seeing Pendra's stunning smooth shiny blue scales and her majestic movements amplified by Kadien's smooth fiery orange scales and sharp elegant moves made Cato find some comfort. As his nightmares were filled with the memories of seeing other stunning dragons ripped to pieces and slaughtered by the orks from his army days. At least these two dragons were safe.

Turning his head Cato managed to see Caden's stunning crystal blue eyes and that wonderful blond hair in the darkness as a cold wind blow past. Making the hair on his arms stand up. Could he go to Caden for warmth?

Cato bit his tongue at that thought. That was inappropriate and he partly hated himself for thinking like this on a mission or potential mission. He needed to focus.

However, this entire thing was a bit strange. But did the Baroness need the Lord Dragon Rider?

Cato really hoped this trip was worth it. He had left the facility centre in the hands of the Chief Hospitaler who Cato had to admit was an amazing Dragon rider herself before she became a healer. She was a friend of his father's and a good leader. So hopefully the centre would be okay for a few hours?

The sound of high heels hitting the hard cold rock under the straw made Cato and the others turn to see the Baroness walk towards him. Cato wanted to shake his head at her choice of clothing since she was wearing a posh black silk dress and probably six-inch heels with a range of jewellery on her. If he was the Baroness he probably would have put on some peasant clothes to avoid being seen. Did she want to be attacked and robbed?

When the Baroness got closer, the moonlight highlighted her well-aged features and Cato would smell her foul flowery perfume. He didn't want to be here too long.

"Baroness Lawic," Cato greeted with a bow.

"My Lord, how is your father?"

"Your father?" Caden interrupted.

The Baroness looked like she was about to tell Caden who his father was but Cato silenced her with a look.

"Why did you request our presence? The last time we spoke you made our feelings known to me about my life choices,"

Cato smiled a little as he heard Pendra rose up and show her rows upon rows of dagger-like teeth to the Baroness.

"Um, yes, my Lord. A past mistake. I summoned you here because my men reported that you're looking into the Ork threat. I have sent messages to the Capital but it will time for them to arrive,"

Pendra took a step closer towards Lawic.

The Baroness' old knees started to shake.

"Baroness, you might have been appointed by the King but even I cannot stop my dragon from eating you. Why have you summoned us?"

"As I mentioned in my letter, my Lord. My Dragon Tea has been stolen by bandits and my men inform me they will sell it to the orks,"

Caden took a step forward.

"Why is that important? In my army days Dragon tea was a myth. It doesn't even do what's it meant to. It can't open portals and anything,"

The sound of harsh dragon laughter made Cato turn to see both dragons rolling around on the floor laughing. Cato had to agree.

"What?"

"My dearest Caden, I need to teach you about the ways of the world,"

Caden gave Cato a boyish smile.

Cato ignored him.

"Dragon Tea is made from an extremely rare type of fungi that feasts on a dragon's corpse and it can in fact open portals and do some other stuff. But it's so rare so no one knows all of its abilities,"

Caden nodded.

"So ya Lawic, ya want us to get ya tea back," Pendra spoke.

Cato rolled his eyes as Lawic's face turned to shock as she realised that Pendra wasn't as majestic as she appeared when she spoke.

"That dragon is not a worthy companion of you, my Lord. She's common,"

Cato stood very close to her. He could feel her body warmth and smell her disgusting perfume.

"You will apologise to my dragon now. You will tell us where these bandits are. I know your men are weak so they will not kill the bandits themselves. Then you will tell me how you got the Dragon Tea. Do you understand?"

She nodded.

Cato was about to step away when the Baroness grabbed his arm.

Pendra and the others took a few steps forward.

He raised his arm to stop them from attacking.

"I would be wary of that man you keep, my Lord. You do not know what he did so watch your back,"

"Is that all?" Cato whispered firmly.

"My Lord don't waste your time with men. It's unholy, unnatural. Where has it got you?"

"All I have to do is wave my arm and Pendra will eat you. Release me,"

She released Cato and he walked back over to the others.

"My Lord, I am sorry for my comments Pendra. The bandits are five miles east in the large cave. I got the Dragon Tea from a pile of Dragon corpses ten miles south," the Baroness said.

Cato's eyes narrowed at the woman as he remembered a time where she had hit both him and his sister hard when they were visiting a decade ago for simply being young people. Laughing, playing games and being young. It never sat right with him or his sister.

Although, he did remember his sister was now something to be with the investigative arm of the people who ran the delivery dragons. Maybe he would tell her about the Baroness shipping Dragon Tea across the land. Even if it was a lie, it would hurt this foul woman's reputation.

He wasn't going to let Lawic go unpunished for her insults and probable crimes but this was not the time. Yet there would be a reckoning.

***

Looking over the edge of the large boulder in front of him, Cato's eyes narrowed as he focused on the cave in front of him. The cave wasn't impressive at all. It was rather boring in fact. The edges of the cave were smooth from what Cato could see. Then the crackling fire of the bandits showed the cave only went back a few metres.

Cato knew this was going to be easy. There were only ten bandits dressed in disgusting, dirty peasant clothes and armed with a few rusty swords.

The sound of the fire crackling echoed around the cave and that made it sound loud behind the boulder where Cato and the others were hiding.

One benefit Cato supposed was the air smelt of crispy boar meat and fresh herbs. Meaning the bandits were almost certainly focusing on their dinner too much to notice them. That was his hope at least.

Even if he was not, he wasn't worried. He had two dragons and the beautiful Caden. Failure was not possible he hoped. All they needed to do what attack the bandits and recover the Dragon Tea. How hard could that be?

Turning around to see the others, Cato almost laughed as he saw the two beautiful dragons attempting badly to crouch on the thick forest floor as the wind blew through the trees. Making Cato's skin cold.

Then for some reason Pendra decided to place a few leaves over her eyes for added camouflage. Cato rolled his eyes and knew he needed to teach her how human sight worked.

As the wind continued to blow and made the tree branches smashed into each other overhead. Cato shivered a little and Caden put his arm over him.

With Caden's beautiful body warmth seeping into his thin armour, Cato really didn't want this to end but they had a mission to do. Yet Cato felt his stomach churn a little at the thought of something happening to Caden. It had happened before on a mission, and he hated the feeling. He couldn't let it happen again, but he had a job to do.

He looked around at the others and nodded. Everyone nodded their response.

"For the King!" Cato screamed.

They all jumped over the boulder.

They charged towards the cave.

Cato felt the thick plants being crushed under his feet.

He didn't care.

Cato whipped out his double bladed staff.

The enemy jumped up.

Grabbing whatever they could.

It was too late.

Cato rushed over to the bandits. Swinging his staff.

Their bodies shattered as their flesh and blood were sprayed up the cave walls.

The fire hissed as blood gushed over it.

The fire was no more.

A bandit charged at Cato.

He turned around.

Driving his staff into the bandit's chest.

More bandits charged. Screaming at Cato.

Caden rushed over.

Slaughtering the enemy in strong powerful yet elegant swipes of his swords.

A bandit tackled Cato to the ground.

His bladed staff flew out of his hands.

The bandit smashed her fists into Cato's face.

Blood dripped from Cato's nose.

His vision blurred.

Pain flooded his body from the punches.

The punching stopped.

His vision cleared.

Cato's eyes widened as the bandit's body was ripped to shred by Pendra's teeth.

Cato jumped up. Grabbed a nearby bandit. Snapped her neck.

Caden threw him his bladed staff.

Not many left.

Caden screamed.

Cato spun.

Raged filled his body.

A bandit's sword dripped red his Caden's blood.

Cato screamed. He charged over. Jumping up into the air. Kicking the bandit to the ground.

He landed on top of the bandit.

Cato rammed his staff into the bandit's face.

The bones shattered and crushed as the bladed staff slaughtered him.

An arrow shot into Cato's back.

He whipped around.

The archer prepared to fire.

Cato launched his staff at the archer.

The staff went straight through the archer.

Blood gushed to the floor. Creating a great pool of the dark red liquid.

The sound of blades clashing made Cato turn.

Caden sliced off one of the bandit's arms. Before he got him into a headlock and snapped his neck. The body landed with a loud thud.

Looking at Caden's stunning movements as he bent down to make sure the bandit was dead. Cato could see why he was a former commander. Caden was skilled, a great warrior and beautiful but there was something about his anger that didn't make sense. Maybe Cato would find out one day why he got kicked out of the military, but until then he could only appreciate his fighting skills.

"Catty, where's ya tea?" Pendra asked from the entrance to the cave.

It was only then that Cato realised how small the

opening to the cave was. It definitely wasn't big enough for a dragon to fit through. But she was right.

Looking around, Cato focused on the cave as his body attempted to relax after the fight. There was nothing here except some wild boar meat. Tasty. But not Dragon Tea.

"Cato,"

The Lord Dragon Rider instantly relaxed as Caden's velvety voice said his name.

Walking over to Caden, he passed Cato a piece of parchment from one of the corpses. He read it.

"What is it, Catty?"

Cato stayed silent.

"I think the human is concerned," Kadien said, and Cato had forgotten he was even here.

"What is it?" Caden said as he gently rubbed Cato's arm.

Cato explained, "This is a payment order. The Orks have already bought the shipment of Dragon Tea and they plan on using it tomorrow morning,".

***

Watching Pendra and Kadien attempt to relight the fire was entertainment all by itself. As each dragon attempted to breathe their fire harshly enough to get rid of the blood and dampness on the wood. But gently enough not to destroy the cave.

Cato rolled his eyes as he threw away the last of the wild boar meat that Kadien was annihilated after he mostly filled the entire cave with fire. And of course almost killing Caden and himself in the process.

Still watching the two dragons try and relight the fire, Cato decided to focus on other matters as he felt the wet blood underneath him turn cold. This made chills run across his body as a gentle cold nightly breeze blew past.

A part of him smiled at the cold breeze and cave as it reminded him of a *great* idea his sister had had once. The two of them decided to camp in the wild as children. For one whole night they were both freezing, hungry and alone. Not the best plan and their father was furious when they came back but it was a fun time together. Cato really missed her. He needed to see her soon. But family's rarely that simple.

Then the thought of the Dragon tea came into his mind. They were too late and now thousands might die because of it. If the Orks used that tea then they might summon an army.

It wasn't really the army idea that concerned Cato. Himself, Caden, the dragons and the Dragonlets could easily defend an army of Orks. Or at least hold them until reinforcements arrived.

What concerned him was what else the Orks might bring. The Orks did like their pets and even all those years ago when he was in the military, the Orks had some horrific creations. The reports recently were not promising either. Some reports even suggested they had created some sort of demon dragon.

Cato and Pendra had fought Dark Dragons before and he really did not want to fight anymore. They never ever ended well.

The feeling of a warm rough hand being put over his shoulders made him smile and turn to see Caden come closer to him. Cato really wanted to act on his feelings. And trying so hard to deny them or push them away, he just wanted Caden. He didn't know why. He just did.

A roar of fire erupted as the two dragons finally got the fire working. The immediate warmth was a welcomed feeling to Cato's skin.

Caden was about to move away but Cato rested his head on Caden's strong arms.

"Well done," Cato smiled.

"Thank ya. Thank ya,"

"I apologise for the delay but my fellow dragon was not doing it correctly," Kadien explained.

"It's fine. I've got a job for you both," Cato said.

"What ya want, Catty?"

"You remember Baroness Lawic said she was getting her Dragon Tea from a cave of dragon corpses?"

"Of course. I always remember things," Kadien replied.

"I want one of you to go there and destroy it. We don't need Dragon Tea in the Realm. Too dangerous,"

"I will go and I will not fail,"

Cato always had to smile at Kadien's proudness.

"And the other one, Catty?"

"You my stunning Pendra. Want to hunt some Orks? We need to know where they're staying. We strike tomorrow at dawn?"

Caden placed his mouth near Cato's ear.

"How do you know they won't use the Tea tonight?"

Cato waved a hand to tell the dragons not to laugh.

"Because my dear, Dragon Tea only works when the sun is up,"

"We won't let ya down," Pendra said as he forced his head into the cave.

Cato lent forward and kissed Pendra's smooth cold scaly snout. Before the two dragons left.

Caden moved over to be as close as he could get to Cato and asked: "What are we going to do?"

As much as Cato really, really wanted something to happen. He was a Lord Dragon Rider and a servant of the King.

With extreme reluctance Cato forced himself away from Caden and turned to him.

"Why did you get kicked out?"

"I should ask you the same. And who's your father? Everyone has whispered about him, but they refuse to tell me,"

Cato did enjoy that secret.

"Caden, I'll tell you who my father is if you tell me why you got kicked out? I know it was for treason and murder but you were saved,"

"How do you know that!"

"I checked,"

"With who?"

"The Lord Commander,"

"That…"

"Caden, I'm not your enemy but I need to know,"

"We're known each other for four months now. You must trust me?"

"I do, but I need to know,"

"Fine, I killed ten people. Four were captains and six were brand new soldiers,"

Cato was silent.

"They… they were traitors. I found evidence of them working with a witch cult. They wanted to bring the cultists into our military forces so they could get the witches to the Orks. I don't know why. I confronted them and they attacked me,"

"And your accusations?"

"No one believed me. I found letters going back weeks about the plot. The new soldiers. Two were witches. One- a warlock. The plot was happening,"

"Interesting,"

"I'm sorry?"

"The treason charges?"

"People argued I killed the soldiers to serve the Orks. And someone reported I was gay,"

"Which stirred the pot even more. Yes, I know that all too well,"

"You see I did nothing wrong. I am innocent and loyal to the King and only the King,"

"Witch Cult Interesting,"

"Did you hear me? I confirmed I'm no threat to you Cato,"

"Oh yes, at least I know why my father saved you,"

"Why?"

Cato smiled and looked into Caden's beautiful crystal blue eyes.

"My father is all too familiar with Witch Cults. A report must have reached him in time. He believed you,"

"Who is your father?"

Cato stood up and wandered over to the cave entrance. Staring out over the pitch-black forest in the dead of night.

Caden wondered over.

Cato turned to him and replied: "I am Prince Catoian, son of The King and Heir to the Throne,"

Caden's eyes widened and immediately he sank to his knees.

"My Lord, it is an honour,"

Cato ignored him and returned to looking over the dark forest.

Caden stayed on his knees.

"Rise," Cato uttered.

"I thought your name was just… I don't know. I thought the Prince was with the Elves. And the Prince is gay?"

"Rest assured Caden, I am the Prince, the King is my father and the Princess is my sister. I was with the elves after I was kicked out of the military and my father discovered I was gay. The Royal Code would order for my execution but my father refused. He didn't care. But the religious leaders had learnt of this fact so I was sent to the elves. To work on our diplomatic relations. I did that for a year. I got honoured as an Honourary Lord Elf and my father gave me the Dragon Facility,"

Caden was stunned into silence.

"You can speak to a Prince,"

"Um, why don't you tell people?"

"Because I want people to treat me for me. People walk on eggshells around the Royal Family, and they pamper you too much. I am more than capable of doing things myself,"

Caden nodded before saying: "I almost kissed a Prince. Wow!"

Cato had had enough.

He grabbed Caden pulled him closer. They both wanted this.

The sound of flapping wings returning made Cato push Caden away to both their frustrations.

***

Watching as the disgusting Orks walked about a

large stone circle in the centre of an immense green field, Cato's eyes narrowed as his hate grew for them. He could even smell their foul odour on the strong wind and the smell of raw meat. There was nothing pleasant about this.

Just watching the massive brown humanoid Orks in their stupid armour made Cato's skin crawl and his stomach churn. They were foul beasts.

In the middle of the stone circle laid a strange mound of bright blue, green and pink soil. Then Cato realised that was the Dragon Tea. The Orks were using it and getting it all together.

Cato might not have known how the Dragon Tea worked exactly but he knew he needed to stop it.

The unwanted thought about what happened last night between him and Caden came into this mind. He really liked Caden, perhaps loved him. But this wasn't the time to think about this. And Cato really didn't need his concerns about losing Caden to affect his judgement.

Turning his head slightly, he saw both the stunning dragons were behind him waiting patiently and Caden looked at him. Cato knew he wasn't mad at him for pushing him away, but it didn't stop Cato from feeling bad.

The sound of crackling flames made Cato look at the stone circle.

Massive red, pink and blue flames rose into the sky.

The Orks started chanting and shouting.

The air crackled with magical power and the stone circle hummed to life.

An immense blue tear started to form in reality.

The Orks grew louder and louder like some

dodgy out of tune choir.

All of them didn't hesitate.

Cato and Caden jumped on their dragons.

The dragons flew over to the stone circle.

Cato and Caden jumped off.

Whipping out their blades and staff.

Cato charged at the nearest Ork. Chopping off his head.

Black oily blood sputtered out. Making the ground turn black.

Cato kept hacking through the Orks.

Bones shattered.

Muscles snapped.

Heads crushed under his feet as they fell.

The Orks tried to attack.

It was useless.

Cato thrusted his staff through their armour.

Their organs exploded.

The Orks screamed.

Cato felt his armour warm up from the constant stream of blood pouring over it.

The dragon roared as they attacked the tear in reality.

The other Orks chanted louder and louder.

The Tear shrieked.

Cato covered his ears.

An Ork tackled him. Sinking her teeth into his armour.

Cato screamed in pain.

He forced his staff through her armour.

She bit down harder.

Her teeth chomped through his left arm.

Cato screamed in agony.

Pendra whacked the foul ork off with her tail.

Cato forced himself up.

The tear in reality shrieked as loud as it could.

The Lord Dragon Rider felt his ears bleed.

The tear ripped open. Becoming a portal.

Revealing the foul ash-covered wasteland of the far, far north.

Massive orks jumped through the portal.

The two dragons breathed constant blue torrents of fire at the portal. Forcing the orks back.

Cato slashed the throat of another Ork.

He needed a plan.

A short male Ork whacked Cato from behind. Jumping on his back.

Cato felt something crack.

The Ork grabbed Cato by the back of his neck. Cato felt his cold slimy fingers.

Cato saw a dagger coming through his throat.

He whacked the Ork with his staff.

The ork didn't move.

The dagger flew towards Cato's neck.

Kadien shot a fireball at the Ork.

The immense Orks came through the portal. Their skin was oily black. They started to snap the necks of their weaker friends with their bare hands.

Cato looked at the pit of tea.

He knew what he needed to do.

Cato pointed Kadien to the pit of Tea.

He understood.

He unleashed a torrent of bright yellow fire at the pit.

The portal pulsed.

Pendra joined in.

The tea released massive columns of thick black smoke.

The portal continued to pulse and flash.

Cato lashed more throats as the Orks attacked.

But it was useless. The pit of Tea turned to ash and the portal pulsed a final time before giving an almighty shriek as it closed.

Cato looked at the six-black oily orks that had broken through. They looked like they were going to attack but Pendra whacked them into the air. Then Kadien whacked them into the distance. Making them fly for kilometres.

Looking around it was finally over Cato had completed his task. The Dragon Tea was all destroyed. No orks or weird Baroness could use it for their personal gains.

At least Cato could go back to the training facility with a great story and a report for the trainees and his father.

But as much as Cato wanted to go back to the Facility and train the next generation of Dragon Riders to fight these Orks. He wanted two things more than anything else.

It was only now after fighting orks twice in the space of four months that Cato had realised he had missed this all. He was a warrior, a servant of the King more than anything else. He wanted to fight once again. Cato didn't want to teach anymore. He needed to serve once again.

Then he looked over to the two stunning dragons and the truly beautiful Caden. He wanted him. He really did.

Maybe it was just some fantasy that wouldn't happen, but he thought he might love him and Cato was going to make sure they would be together no matter what. If Caden wanted, of course.

After a few moments, Pendra wandered over to her old friend and lowered her head onto the ground. Cato leaned on her, enjoying the feel of her cold smooth scales against his fingers.

"What now, Catty. The mission is over. Yet we don't wanna go do we?"

"No. I want to see the world. I don't want to be exiled again. I want to serve my father,"

"I'll always be with ya. What about them?" Pendra gestured over to Caden and Kadien.

Cato simply looked over there. Admiring Caden's beautiful longish blond hair and stunning crystal blue eyes.

"Do ya love him?"

"Yes,"

GET YOUR FREE AND EXCLUSIVE SHORT STORY NOW! LEARN ABOUT NEMESIO'S PAST!

https://www.subscribepage.com/fireheart

About the author:

Connor Whiteley is the author of over 60 books in the sci-fi fantasy, nonfiction psychology and books for writer's genre and he is a Human Branding Speaker and Consultant.

He is a passionate warhammer 40,000 reader, psychology student and author.

Who narrates his own audiobooks and he hosts The Psychology World Podcast.

All whilst studying Psychology at the University of Kent, England.

Also, he was a former Explorer Scout where he gave a speech to the Maltese President in August 2018 and he attended Prince Charles' 70th Birthday Party at Buckingham Palace in May 2018.

Plus, he is a self-confessed coffee lover!

OTHER SHORT STORIES BY CONNOR WHITELEY

Blade of The Emperor
Arbiter's Truth
The Bloodied Rose
Asmodia's Wrath
Heart of A Killer
Emissary of Blood
Computation of Battle
Old One's Wrath
Puppets and Masters
Ship of Plague
Interrogation
Edge of Failure
One Way Choice
Acceptable Losses
Balance of Power
Good Idea At The Time
Escape Plan
Escape In The Hesitation
Inspiration In Need
Singing Warriors
Dragon Coins
Dragon Tea
Dragon Rider
Knowledge is Power
Killer of Polluters
Climate of Death
Sacrifice of the Soul
Heart of The Flesheater

Heart of The Regent
Heart of The Standing
Feline of The Lost
Heart of The Story
The Family Mailing Affair
Defining Criminality
The Martian Affair
A Cheating Affair
The Little Café Affair
Mountain of Death
Prisoner's Fight
Claws of Death
Bitter Air
Honey Hunt
Blade On A Train
City of Fire
Awaiting Death
Poison In The Candy Cane
Christmas Innocence
You Better Watch Out
Christmas Theft
Trouble In Christmas
Smell of The Lake
Problem In A Car
Theft, Past and Team

Other books by Connor Whiteley:

The Fireheart Fantasy Series
Heart of Fire
Heart of Lies
Heart of Prophecy
Heart of Bones
Heart of Fate

City of Assassins (Urban Fantasy)
City of Death
City of Marytrs
City of Pleasure
City of Pleasure

Agents of The Emperor
Return of The Ancient Ones
Vigilance
Angels of Fire

The Garro Series- Fantasy/Sci-fi
GARRO: GALAXY'S END
GARRO: RISE OF THE ORDER
GARRO: END TIMES
GARRO: SHORT STORIES
GARRO: COLLECTION
GARRO: HERESY
GARRO: FAITHLESS
GARRO: DESTROYER OF WORLDS
GARRO: COLLECTIONS BOOK 4-6

GARRO: MISTRESS OF BLOOD
GARRO: BEACON OF HOPE
GARRO: END OF DAYS

<u>Winter Series- Fantasy Trilogy Books</u>
WINTER'S COMING
WINTER'S HUNT
WINTER'S REVENGE
WINTER'S DISSENSION

<u>Miscellaneous:</u>
RETURN
FREEDOM
SALVATION

www.ingramcontent.com/pod-product-compliance
Lightning Source LLC
LaVergne TN
LVHW020501080526
838202LV00057B/6089